Ghost Dog

Ghost Dog

by Eleanor Allen

Interior illustrations by Neal McPheeters
Cover illustration by David Gaadt

A
LITTLE APPLE
PAPERBACK

SCHOLASTIC INC.
New York   Toronto   London   Auckland   Sydney

ISBN 0-590-16369-8

Text copyright © 1996 by Eleanor Allen.
Illustrations copyright © 1997 by Scholastic Inc.
Cover illustration by David Gaadt.
All rights reserved. Published by Scholastic Inc.,
555 Broadway, New York, NY 10012
by arrangement with Scholastic Ltd.
LITTLE APPLE PAPERBACKS and logos are trademarks of Scholastic Inc.
SCHOLASTIC and associated logos are trademarks
and/or registered trademarks of Scholastic Inc.

10 9 8 7 6

Printed in the U.S.A.   40

First American edition, October 1997

For Lucy

Ghost
Dog

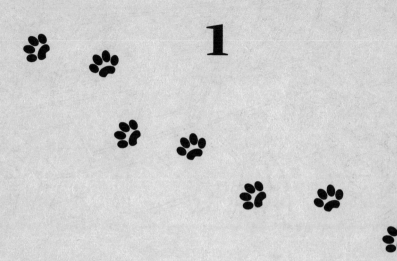

1

Kim Martin and her mom and dad lived in a big city. Their apartment was at the very top of a tall, narrow house with winding stairs. At the back of the house was a damp little yard, where the garbage cans were kept. Along the pavement, shoppers' feet, shoppers' carts, and shoppers' strollers jostled past in the hundreds every day.

"Not a place to keep a dog," said Mom.

"Nowhere to walk a dog," nodded Dad. "It would howl with boredom and disturb the neighbors."

"Foul the sidewalk," shuddered Mom.

"A one hundred dollar fine," said Dad.

"Not fair to a dog," they said.

"But I want a dog," said Kim. "More than anything in the world, I want a dog."

To make it up to her, they gave Kim

stuffed dogs; china dogs; wooden dogs; mechanical dogs — every sort of dog you can think of that wasn't *real*. They bought her posters of dogs for her walls and filled her shelves with books on dogs.

"Not to worry. She'll soon grow out of it," said Mom.

"She'll have to," said Dad. "A real dog's impossible, while we're living here. . . ."

But one day, the Martins' lifestyle changed. Dad got a new job. They left the cramped apartment on the top floor of the tall, narrow house in the busy city. They moved to a little house that stood all alone in a big garden at the end of a street. Beyond the garden was a field and beyond the field was a little woods. It was the perfect place for a dog.

And a dog had lived there, once.

The day they moved in, Mrs. Martin complained that the house smelled of dog. She went to the supermarket for air

freshener. She scrubbed and rescrubbed the floors. In the garden shed, where Dad was putting his brand-new lawnmower, he found a worn and rusty sign that said BEWARE OF THE DOG. And on the back door, Kim found old scratch marks, deeply gouged.

"Can I have my dog now?" Kim asked.

"Wait until we've settled in," said Mom. "There's too much going on right now to think about dogs."

That night, as she lay in bed in her bare, new room, Kim thought she heard a dog barking and howling. It sounded close by. She climbed out of bed to investigate.

The room seemed dark without the friendly orange glow from neon street-lights. And when she pulled back the curtain, the garden wasn't daytime friendly anymore. It was deeply shadowy and murkily mysterious and the branches of the trees made weird and tortured shapes

against the sky. From behind a cloud, the moon winked with an evil face. Instead of cheery voices and footsteps and banging car doors and roaring engines and the urgent WOW-WOW, WOW-WOW of police cars, there was no sound at all but the low, lonesome moaning of the wind in the trees.

Kim shivered. She scurried back to bed and pulled the comforting quilt over her head.

If only there *had* been a dog in the garden! she thought. A big, friendly dog to keep guard over them while they slept . . .

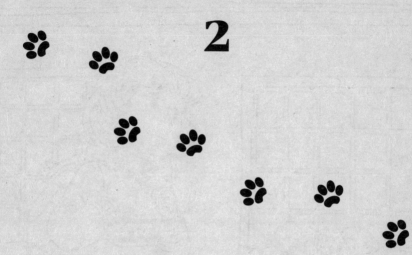

2

Next day, Kim started at her new school. It was in the village, a good mile away. Compared to her old school, it was very small. All the children seemed to know each other, like a big, close family to which she did not belong. They stared at Kim and giggled, and muttered things about her behind their hands. Kim felt more like an alien from outer space than a newcomer from the city.

"How was your new school?" Mr. Martin asked when he returned from work. Kim told him no one seemed to like her there. And it was an awful long way to walk, there and back, every day.

"Oh, dear," said Dad. "It isn't nice to feel left out. But after a while you'll be one of the gang, I'm sure you will."

"They just need time to get to know you, Kim," said Mom. "You'll soon make friends. Just wait and see."

"We could solve the other problem now, though," said Dad. "We could get her a bike to ride to school on. The roads around here are very safe."

"Good idea," nodded Mom.

"Great!" cried Kim. She cheered up quite a bit. She had always wanted a bike, but the roads were too dangerous in the city.

"Are *you* settling in all right?" Mr. Martin asked his wife.

"Well, it's very quiet here, after the

city," she said. "But I expect I'll get used to it. I can't seem to get rid of that dog smell, though. It's worst in the kitchen and the living room, near the fireplace.

"Are we settled in enough to talk about *my* dog yet?" Kim asked. A bike was very good, but a dog would be even better.

A dog that would meet her from school with a wagging tail and listen to her troubles. A dog that would be her friend.

"Don't pester," said Mom. "We've just promised you a bike. And with a dog there's a lot to think about."

"Like what?"

"Like the new carpet that's being fitted tomorrow," said Dad. "It costs a lot of money. We don't want a new puppy wee-ing all over it."

"Or an older dog running across it with great muddy paws," added Mom.

"It could sleep in the kitchen," said Kim. "And have a doghouse outside in the daytime. The back garden's perfect for a dog."

"Hmmm. That may well be," said Mom. "But who would look after it when we go back to the city to visit Grandma and Grandpa?"

"And I was thinking of putting some flower beds in the garden," said Dad. "I wouldn't want them dug up. A dog needs some serious thinking about, Kim. Give us time."

Kim stomped off to her room.
Excuses, excuses!
She put up all her dog posters on the walls, unpacked the dog books, and arranged all the fluffy dogs, wooden dogs, and china dogs on the bed, on the chest of drawers, and on the window ledge. It looked just like her old room.

Then Kim was hit by a dreadful feeling. Supposing her parents went right on making excuses? Supposing, deep down, they didn't like dogs? Supposing they never intended to get her a real *live* dog — one that she could love and that would love her back. . . .

Kim started to cry. But suddenly, the smell of dog wafted in her nostrils. Something warm and furry seemed to brush against her legs. There was nothing to be seen, but Kim's tears dried up. She felt strangely excited and comforted.

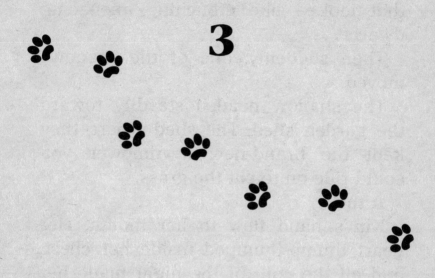

3

That night, Kim thought she heard the barking again. She sat up in bed and listened. This time it seemed close by, as though it was coming from the garden.

She opened the window and peered out. The air smelled country-chill and damp and full of vegetation. The lawn was a sea of silvery-gray and across it, the bushes and shrubs of the borders cast spooky black shadows. Shadows that looked like crouching, menacing dwarfs . . .

Then suddenly, one of the shadows moved.

The shadow headed steadily toward the garden shed. The shed where they kept the brand-new lawnmower you could ride on to cut the grass.

A thief!

Kim's hand flew to her mouth. Her heart thump-thumped inside her chest, and all the chill of the night made her shiver. She wanted to run to her parents' room, to shout for help, but her legs wouldn't move and fear lodged in her throat like a lump of apple.

And then another shadow moved. Crouching low, it moved menacingly across the lawn toward the figure. And as it moved, it growled — a deep, ferocious, threatening growl.

The figure stopped and jerked around. It flung up startled arms and shouted. Then suddenly the thief turned and fled. Back down the garden the figure raced, and over the fence it flung itself, with the shadow dog right behind him. The fence shook as the shadow dog leaped against it, flinging back its head and firing off a string of barks that split the air like bullets.

Kim forgot her fear. She clapped her hands. "Brave dog! You chased him away!" she shouted. "Good dog — you saved our lawnmower! And Dad's new garden tools!"

The shadow dog threw one last bark, then trotted back across the lawn toward the house. Beneath Kim's window the

dog stopped, sat down on its haunches, and looked up at her.

Kim could see the dog clearly now. It was a big dog. A very big, black dog.

She shivered with excitement.

"Do you want to come in?" she called.

The dog barked eagerly.

"Shh . . ." she said. "I'm coming down."

Carefully, Kim drew back the bolt on the door. A cold breeze spiraled through the house as she opened it.

"Here, boy," she whispered, and looked out and waited.

Nothing entered.

"Here, boy," she whispered again. "Don't be shy, I won't hurt you."

She heard a whimper. But surprisingly, it came from behind her.

There, sitting by the kitchen sink, was the big, black dog. Its wide, domed head was cocked expectantly.

Kim did a double-take. "How did you get there?" she asked.

She could see the whole sink unit, though the dog was sitting in front of it. The dog was see-through!

She stifled a scream.

The dog moved anxiously. It sensed her alarm. Its large brown eyes stared at her pleadingly and its tail thumped gently on the floor. "Don't give me away," it seemed to be saying. "I mean you no harm."

"I'm scared of you," Kim whispered.

The dog whined softly. It raised a paw and offered it.

Despite her fear, Kim smiled. The dog seemed to smile back. Its eyes shone and its tongue hung out of its mouth. Kim knew it was a good dog. Not a dog to be afraid of — except that it was a ghost dog!

4

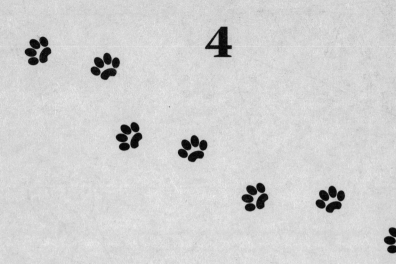

Over the next few days, Kim and the ghost dog became friends. She kept him secret from her parents. They could smell him, but they never saw him. He only appeared for Kim, when nobody else was there. He would wait by the garden gate to greet her when she rode home from school. They would go for a walk along the street and she would tell him all her troubles.

Sometimes, as she was eating her dinner, or watching TV with her parents, she would feel his warm body brushing against her legs, or his smooth pink tongue licking her hand. It felt good to know he was still there, even when she couldn't see him.

She named her ghost dog Rex. The name came into her mind one day. And when she said it, he wagged his tail as though he knew it.

Rex was kind and as gentle as a lamb, but he was a good guard dog. Guarding the house and garden was his job. He took it very seriously. If a stranger walked along the lane, Kim would glimpse Rex, lying in wait behind the hedge, ready to bark at the first sign of trouble.

One day, Kim's mother was looking anxious. "The milkman tells me there have been some break-ins around here lately. We need to be more careful. We shouldn't leave doors unlocked and windows open, or the place unguarded."

Another day she said, "I was down at the bottom of the garden, weeding. I thought I heard a dog barking inside the house. I came up the garden to investigate — and do you know what? The postman was ringing the doorbell, with a package. I'd have missed him if I hadn't thought I'd heard a dog. If it had been a robber, instead of the postman, he could have stolen all we have and I wouldn't have heard a thing."

Kim longed to tell her mother that the barking dog was Rex and that Rex was always on guard. But she knew Rex had to be kept a secret.

Gradually, Kim began to settle down in her new school. School didn't seem so bad, now that she had her ghost dog friend at home. She looked forward to telling him all that had happened every day.

Mr. Martin was enjoying his new job. But Mom was feeling lonely in the new house. She missed all her neighbors in the city and she missed the noise. Now she was always worried that a thief might break into the house.

"That dog smell's still here, isn't it?" said Dad one evening.

"I don't notice it now," Mom said. "I must have gotten used to it."

"I was wondering," continued Dad, "maybe we should think about getting that dog for Kim. It would be a friend for her and a companion for you. And I'm not getting enough exercise, now that I don't play tennis. It would be nice to go for a walk sometimes. But I don't like to go on my own. A dog would be a good excuse."

"I'd like a dog to guard the house and keep me company," said Mom. "The milk-

man tells me there's been another burglary in town. I'd like a puppy that I could train."

"What about the new carpet?" asked Dad.

"We could keep the puppy in the kitchen until it was housebroken."

"Then it could have a doghouse outside."

"The back garden's perfect for a dog."

Kim could not believe her ears.

"We know how much you've always wanted a dog, Kim. It would be your dog," they said.

Poor Rex! Kim thought — how would he feel? The house and garden were his. He guarded them. What would he do if a puppy arrived?

"But who would look after it when we go to the city to visit Grandma and Grandpa?" she asked in despair. "And what about the flower beds?"

Her parents smiled. "We'll sort that out

when the time comes," they said. "Just think — a dog of your very own, at last!"

Kim forced a delighted smile. She could never explain that she had a dog already. A ghost dog.

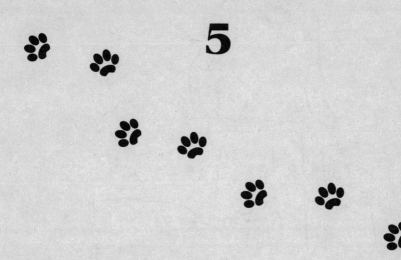

5

A day or two later, when Dad arrived home, he was carrying a large, cardboard box. Inside it was the wiggliest, chubbiest, most adorable puppy you could imagine.

He captured everyone's hearts. Kim named the puppy Bobby. It seemed a round and bouncing sort of name, and this was a very round and bouncing sort of dog.

It should have been the happiest day of Kim's life. But deep inside, she felt miserable. This wasn't fair to Rex.

"I'm sorry, Rex," she whispered. "It's not my fault."

She put out her hand, but Rex didn't lick it.

She was afraid Rex was sulking.

That night, Kim could hear the puppy whimpering in its basket in the kitchen. It was feeling lonely.

"It will whimper for a night or two," her mom had warned. "He misses his brothers and sisters and his mom."

But suddenly the whimpering stopped. It stopped so suddenly, Kim felt she ought to check.

She pushed open the kitchen door and peered toward the basket. The basket was overflowing with dog. In it lay Rex, or rather the half of him that would fit in it. And snuggled up against him, snoring peacefully, was Bobby.

"What a good dog you are, Rex," Kim whispered.

Though Mr. and Mrs. Martin never knew it, Rex took over Bobby's upbringing. He taught him how to sit and stay and how to walk properly. He removed him from the best armchair and stopped him from digging up the flower beds. Most important of all, Rex taught him how to be on guard.

"What an intelligent little pup Bobby is!" Mrs. Martin would exclaim. "No sooner have I explained things than he seems to understand. Never once has he wet on the new carpet. And no stranger ever gets beyond the garden gate without a warning bark."

"You must be a very good trainer," said Mr. Martin.

Only Kim knew the truth. Bobby was not an especially intelligent puppy, nor was Mrs. Martin particularly good at training him. It was Rex who deserved all the praise. With the greatest patience in the world, it was Rex who put the puppy through its lessons. And Mr. and Mrs. Martin never knew about the sock that was chewed to bits, or the mug that was shattered. Rex carried away the evidence and buried it behind the garden shed.

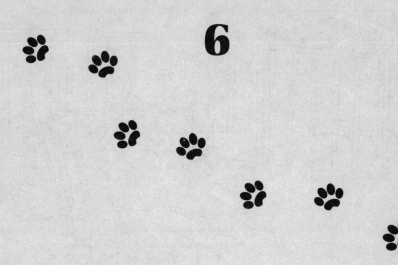

6

As the months passed by, Bobby grew and grew. He grew not only in size, but also in confidence. He was a lovable and affectionate dog, but he was becoming a little cocky.

One afternoon after school, Kim was sitting on the back lawn with her mom. Rex, invisible, was lying at Kim's feet, relaxing because it was Bobby's turn for guard duty.

Suddenly there came a dreadful barking and snarling from the front garden. Rex gave a ghostly, throaty growl and leaped to his feet, quickly followed by Kim, then Mom.

"My bike!" cried Kim. "I left it just inside the gate! I meant to move it, but I forgot."

The garden gate was swinging wide. Twenty feet or so along the street lay Kim's bike, abandoned. Up the street the thief fled, with Bobby at his heels, barking.

"What a brave and clever guard dog you are!" cried Mrs. Martin, when Bobby trotted back.

Kim felt very proud of Bobby, and so did Rex. Rex had taught him so well, he had proved he could now take charge all on his own.

Mr. Martin took the old BEWARE OF THE DOG sign from the shed. He cleaned it up. Kim, Bobby, and Rex watched as he proudly nailed it back in place.

That night, Kim heard Rex barking beneath her bedroom window. She opened the window and called to him. He was sitting on the lawn, looking up at her, just like the first night they had met. But this time, Kim knew he wasn't asking to come in. Rex had come to say good-bye.

He barked three times — short, sharp barks. Then he faded back into the dark shadows.

Kim knew that she would never see him again. He wasn't needed anymore. The house and the garden he had protected so faithfully could now be left in the capable paws of his successor, Bobby.

Kim understood. She knew Rex was happy to go. And she had her real, live dog at last — one she loved and who loved her back.

But a tear ran sadly down her cheek. She knew she would never forget the big, black friendly ghost dog she had known as Rex.

Pony Pals®

Be a Pony Pal®!

Anna, Pam, and Lulu want you to join them on adventures with their favorite ponies!

Order now and you get a free pony portrait bookmark and two collecting cards in all the books—for you *and* your pony pal!

❑ BBC48583-0	#1	I Want a Pony	$2.99
❑ BBC48584-9	#2	A Pony for Keeps	$2.99
❑ BBC48585-7	#3	A Pony in Trouble	$2.99
❑ BBC48586-5	#4	Give Me Back My Pony	$2.99
❑ BBC25244-5	#5	Pony to the Rescue	$2.99
❑ BBC25245-3	#6	Too Many Ponies	$2.99
❑ BBC54338-5	#7	Runaway Pony	$2.99
❑ BBC54339-3	#8	Good-bye Pony	$2.99
❑ BBC62974-3	#9	The Wild Pony	$2.99
❑ BBC62975-1	#10	Don't Hurt My Pony	$2.99
❑ BBC86597-8	#11	Circus Pony	$2.99
❑ BBC86598-6	#12	Keep Out, Pony!	$2.99
❑ BBC86600-1	#13	The Girl Who Hated Ponies	$2.99
❑ BBC86601-X	#14	Pony-Sitters	$3.50
❑ BBC86632-X	#15	The Blind Pony	$3.50
❑ BBC37459-1	#16	The Missing Pony Pal	$3.50
❑ BBC74210-8		Pony Pals Super Special #1: The Baby Pony	$5.99
❑ BBC86631-1		Pony Pals Super Special #2: The Lives of our Ponies	$5.99
❑ BBC37461-3		Pony Pals Super Special #3: The Ghost Pony	$5.99

Available wherever you buy books, or use this order form.

Send orders to Scholastic Inc., P.O. Box 7500, Jefferson City, MO 65102

Please send me the books I have checked above. I am enclosing $_____ (please add $2.00 to cover shipping and handling). Send check or money order — no cash or C.O.D.s please.

Please allow four to six weeks for delivery. Offer good in the U.S.A. only. Sorry, mail orders are not available to residents in Canada. Prices subject to change.

Name_____ Birthdate ____/____/____

Address_____

City_____ State_____ Zip_____

Telephone (   ) _____ ❑ Boy ❑ Girl

Where did you buy this book? ❑ Bookstore ❑ Book Fair ❑ Book Club ❑ Other

PP497

LITTLE  APPLE®

Here are some of our favorite Little Apples.

Once you take a bite out of a Little Apple book—you'll want to read more!

Books for Kids with BIG Appetites!